This book belongs to

_____

_____

_____

For Poppy
–L.J.

For Mum and Dad
–T.W.

tiger tales
an imprint of ME Media, LLC
202 Old Ridgefield Road, Wilton, CT 06897
This edition published in the United States 2003
First published in the United States 1995
by Little Brown and Company
Originally published in Great Britain 1995
by Little Tiger Press
An imprint of Magi Publications
Text ©1995 Linda Jennings
Illustrations ©1995 Tim Warnes
CIP data is available
ISBN 1-58925-383-3
Printed in Singapore

TOM'S TAIL

by
Linda Jennings

Illustrated by
Tim Warnes

tiger tales

Tom's tail was curly like a rolled-up rubber band. It was a very neat little tail for a piglet, but Tom thought it looked silly.

In all other ways Tom
was a proper little pig.

He was a nice pale pink with dirty patches where
he had wallowed in mud. He slurped and snuffled in
the pig trough with his brothers and sisters and made
all the usual piggy noises.

But how he wished he had a straight tail!

Sam the sheepdog
had a lovely, furry tail.

Henry the
horse had a long,
swishy tail.

And Betsy the cow had a thin, stringy tail with a little tuft on the end.

"Even the rat's tail is nicer than mine," said Tom sadly.

"Why don't you get your tail straightened?" said Henry.

"How?" asked Tom.

"Like this," said Henry as he put a big hoof on the end of Tom's tail. "Now walk away."

Tom squealed and squeaked as he began to walk...

His tail stretched out and, when it had uncurled all the way, Henry lifted his hoof.

Ping!

Back sprang the tail...

and Tom hurtled forward...

"Ouch!" yelled Tom and Sam together.

"I'll tell you what," said Sam, picking himself up. "Why don't I take hold of your tail and you can lead me along. That should straighten it out!"

So Tom took Sam for a walk, past the pigsty...

around the pond . . .

and over the buttercup field.
"That's enough!" squealed
Tom. "Let me go!"

ping!

Back sprang the tail to its usual curly self. Tom felt sad.

Betsy looked at Tom,
and chewed thoughtfully.
Suddenly she had a very
good idea. She told Sam . . .

who took hold of Tom's tail again and stretched it. Then he pushed the tail into a big patch of gooey, sticky mud! He made Tom lie with his tail covered in mud for a very long time, until ...

the mud dried, and Tom's tail
was set into a long, thin pencil.
"Yippee!" cried Tom.

He twirled around, trying to see his new straight tail. "Ouch!" said Sam. Tom's pointy tail had poked him in the chest.

"You look so silly," said Tom's mother. But
Tom liked looking different from the other pigs.
"I'll wag my tail like Sam does," he said.
Whack! Tom's tail hit his sister in the face and
then poked his brother's behind.
"Stop it, Tom!" they both shouted.

When it was dark, Tom's mother gathered in all her piglets for the night. They liked to snuggle up in a big heap. But Tom's tail got in the way.

"Go away!" cried all Tom's brothers and sisters,
and they chased him right out of the pigsty.

Poor Tom! He tried to curl up outside but it wasn't
very comfortable to lie down with a tail as stiff as
a pencil. Finally, though, he was able to fall asleep.

During the night it began to rain, but Tom went on sleeping.

As it rained, the hard mud softened and slid off Tom's tail.

By the time morning came, his tail was as curly as it had ever been. Grunting happily, Tom went back to the pigsty.

"Who wants a straight tail anyway?"
said Tom later, as he pushed into the
trough with his brothers and sisters.

"Now if I had a long, elegant nose like Henry the horse instead of this silly, stumpy snout, I could really get at that food!"

Laura's Star
by Klaus Baumgart
ISBN 1-58925-374-4

Pedro the Brave
by Leo Broadley
illustrated by Holly Swain
ISBN 1-58925-375-2

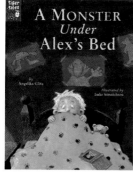

A Monster Under Alex's Bed
by Angelika Glitz
illustrated by Imke Sönnichsen
ISBN 1-58925-373-6

Explore the world of tiger tales!

More fun-filled and exciting stories await you!
Look for these titles and more at your local library or bookstore.
And have fun reading!

tiger tales

202 Old Ridgefield Road, Wilton, CT 06897

The Very Lazy Ladybug
by Isobel Finn
illustrated by Jack Tickle
ISBN 1-58925-379-5

Snarlyhissopus
by Alan MacDonald
illustrated by Louise Voce
ISBN 1-58925-370-1

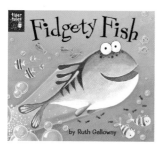

Fidgety Fish
by Ruth Galloway
ISBN 1-58925-377-9